This story is adapted from **Hikayat Sha'biyya min Al-Khalij**
published in 1994 by the Centre of Folk Literature, Doha, Qatar

This book would not have been possible without the generous support of

Published in 2006 by JERBOA BOOKS
PO BOX 333838 Dubai UAE
www.jerboabooks.com
ISBN 9948-431-00-6

Deenoh and Arbab

A Tale of Two Goats

Denys Johnson-Davies

Illustrations Sabine P Moser

One boiling hot day a goat was left all on her own, while her owners went off to see some friends. Before the family came home again, the goat had given birth to two little goats which she named Deenoh and Arbab.

The mother goat was very careful and each time she went out she warned her children not to let anyone into the paddock, where they lived, without making quite sure who it was.

She would then go out early in the morning and wouldn't return until the end of the day, carrying some grass on her horns as food for her children. She also, of course, fed them with her own milk.

When the mother goat reached
the door to the paddock, she
would always call out:

'Deenoh, Deenoh
and Arbab!
Open up the door for your
mother, who is carrying
grass on her horns for her
two little children.'

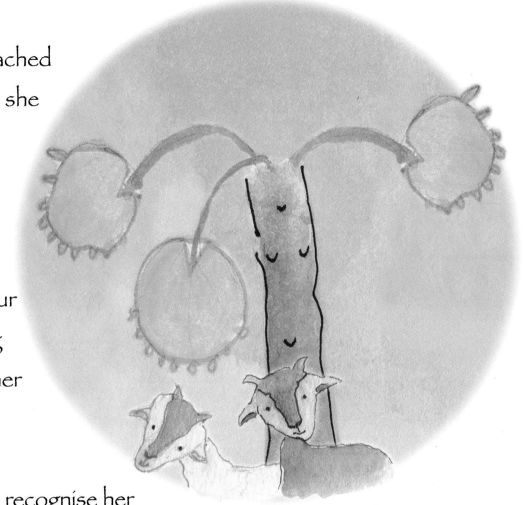

The two little goats would recognise her
voice and would immediately open the door to
let her in so that they could eat the grass and drink her milk.

Then the little goats would settle down next to their mother and go to sleep.

It so happened that there were no less than seven witches who lived nearby, and one of them had been watching the mother goat's movements very closely.

One morning the witch came up to the door of the paddock and knocked on it, hoping she would be let in.

The two little goats realised that it wasn't their mother and refused to open the door, just as they had been taught.

The witch had to go away, but she was angry and was determined not to be defeated, so she returned several days later. This time, the cunning witch knocked at the door, after which she called out:

'Deenoh, Deenoh and Arbab!
Open up the door for your mother, who is carrying grass on her horns for her two little children.'

The two young goats thought they recognised their mother's voice and opened the door to the witch, who sprang at the two little goats and gobbled them up.

The mother goat returned to the paddock at sunset and called out to her two children, expecting them to open the door for her. When there was no answer, she broke down the door and went into the paddock.

She couldn't believe her eyes when she found the paddock empty, and she quickly realised that one of the seven wicked witches must be responsible for the disappearance of her two children.

Immediately the mother goat set out, to where she knew the seven witches lived. They were all preparing their evening meal and each one of the witches had a pot cooking over a fire.

She went up to the first witch and knocked over her cooking pot.

'Who dares to knock over my cooking pot when I'm preparing supper for my little ones?' shouted the first witch.

The mother goat replied, 'It was me, who knocked over your cooking pot, and it is me who wants to know who has eaten my little ones?'

The first witch swore she had nothing to do with the disappearance of the goat's children, so the mother goat went to the second witch, then to the third witch, and to the fourth, and the fifth and the sixth. They all swore that they were not responsible for anything that might have happened to the mother goat's children.

Finally, the mother goat went to the seventh witch, who was the chief of all the witches. Here again she knocked over the cooking pot, which was on the fire.

'How dare you do that when I'm preparing food for my children?'
said the witch, fuming with rage.

'I dare to do so,' answered the mother goat,
'and I want to know if it is you who has taken my little ones?'

The chief of the witches had to admit she had taken
the little goats.

'Yes, and I've had them for my supper,'
she said, staring at the mother goat.

'And very soon,' she added with a horrible laugh,
'I'll be having their mother too!'

The wicked witch's words struck fear into the heart of the poor mother goat and she was full of anger and hatred. She sprang at the wicked witch and butted her with all her might.

Her horns were long and sharp and they ripped a large hole in the witch's stomach, out of which sprang the two little goats!

The mother goat was extremely happy to find that her children were still alive and she quickly took them back to the safety of their home.

There in the paddock, she fed them and let them drink her milk. Soon, Deenoh and Arbab grew sleepy and curled up beside their mother.

Before they fell asleep their mother once again

gave them a serious warning,

'Be very careful,'

she told them,

'not to open the door to

everyone who knocks or

everyone who calls out.

Always be sure to look and see

who's there. Just to hear is not

enough - you have to see with

your own eyes.'

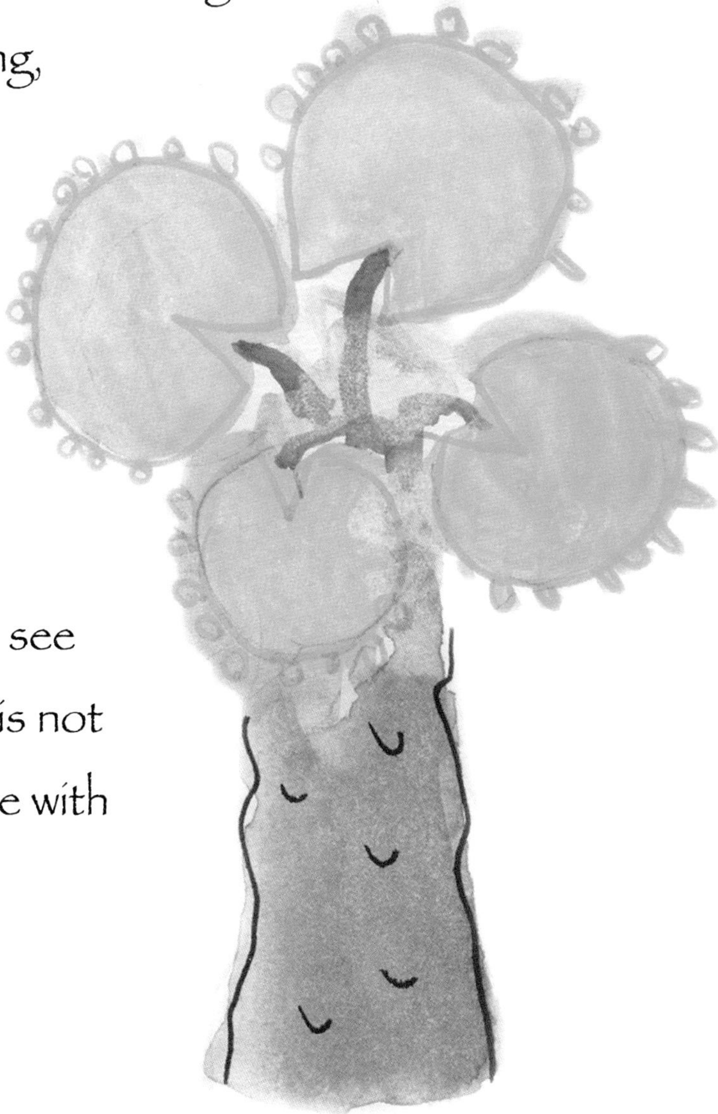

Denys Johnson-Davies has been called 'the pioneer translator of modern Arabic literature'.

He has also made a name for himself as a writer of children's books, of which he has published more than thirty titles.

He lives in Marrakesh, Morocco.

Photograph by Paola Crociani

Sabine P Moser is married, mother of three and a kindergarten teacher.

She recently moved back to Austria, having lived in Dubai from 1999 to 2004.

During her stay she began to write and illustrate stories about an aptly named camel, Camel-O-Shy.

Tales of Arabia

More Tales for you to enjoy!

A Tale from Kuwait

The King and his Three Daughters

The King asks his daughters how much they love him and the answer of his third daughter greatly displeases him. Banished from her home she will later teach her father a valuable lesson when they meet again after many years.

A Tale from Qatar

The Woodcutter

Struggling to feed his family, the woodcutter discovers a genie in a tree in the forest. The genie takes pity on the poor woodcutter, but his foolishness leads him into trouble over and over again. Will he ever learn?

A Tale from Oman

The Great Warrior Ali

Ali's father was a great warrior and Ali wants to be just like him. He's never had any training as a warrior but somehow manages to convince everyone he is a great swordsman. We follow his adventures in this wonderful tale from Oman.